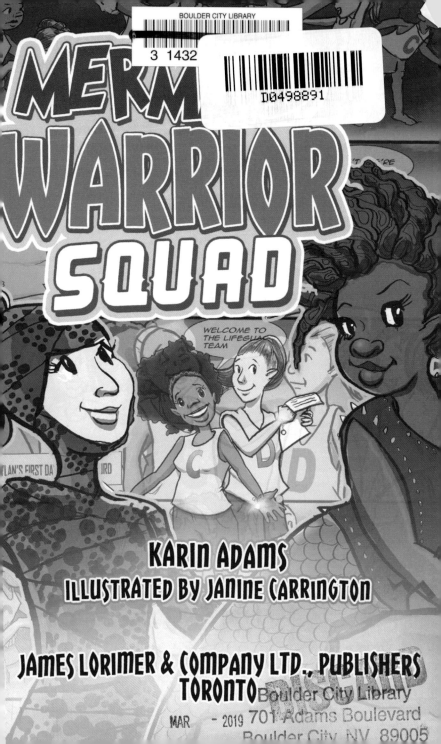

MERM
WARRIOR
SQUAD

KARIN ADAMS
ILLUSTRATED BY JANINE CARRINGTON

JAMES LORIMER & COMPANY LTD., PUBLISHERS
TORONTO

James Lorimer & Company Ltd., Publishers acknowledges funding support from
the Ontario Arts Council (OAC), an agency of the Government of Ontario. We
acknowledge the support of the Canada Council for the Arts, which last year
invested $153 million to bring the arts to Canadians throughout the country. This
project has been made possible in part by the Government of Canada and with the
support of the Ontario Media Development Corporation.

Cover design: Tyler Cleroux
Cover image: Janine Carrington

Library and Archives Canada Cataloguing in Publication

Adams, Karin, author
    Mermaid warrior squad / Karin Adams ; illustrated by
Janine Carrington.

Issued in print and electronic formats.
ISBN 978-1-4594-1146-3 (softcover).--ISBN 978-1-4594-1151-7 (EPUB)

    I. Carrington, Janine, illustrator II. Title.

PS8601.D453M47 2017   jC813'.6   C2017-903294-1
                                               C2017-903295-X

Published by:
James Lorimer &
Company Ltd., Publishers
117 Peter Street, Suite 304
Toronto, ON, Canada
M5V 0M3
www.lorimer.ca

Distributed in Canada by:
Formac Lorimer Books
5502 Atlantic Street
Halifax, NS, Canada
B3H 1G4

Distributed in the US by:
Lerner Publisher Services
1251 Washington Ave. N.
Minneapolis, MN, USA
55401
www.lernerbooks.com

Manufactured by Friesens Corporation in Altona, Manitoba,
Canada in April 2018.
Job #242781

For Annabel and Elanor

CONTENTS

1
DIVE In!

I stared at the wide green lawn in front of the arts college. It was crawling with kids my age, but I didn't know anyone. Everyone was paired up or gathered in groups, like they were best friends. My palms were sweating. Worse, I felt like my yellow, art-camp T-shirt made me stand out. As far as I could see, no one else was wearing one. I had gotten a free shirt in the mail when I registered, and I thought we were all supposed to wear it, at least on the first day. What else did I not know about day camp?

I decided to look busy. That way, everyone might not stare so much. I headed back to the welcome table. My smiley group leader, Kelsey, was still there handing out nametags. Mine was fish-shaped and my name, *Dylan*, was printed on it in bubbly letters. When I got there, I pretended to be interested in the colourful sign stuck to the front of the table. It said, "Welcome to Art Camp: Art Under the Sea!" I looked at the rippling tentacles of a smiling cartoon squid. In case anyone was watching, I pressed my lips together and nodded, like I was in a museum looking at a piece of art.

As I leaned closer to the sign, a booming voice made me jump. "Your necklace is AWESOME!"

Beside me was a girl who looked around eleven, just like me. Stuck to her chest was a nametag that said *Coral*. Her hair was big and curly, and her round face was split by a huge grin. She made me think of a friendly Halloween pumpkin. But best of all — Coral was wearing her bright yellow camp T-shirt too!

"So, is it *really* a shark tooth?" Coral reached out and touched the pointy tooth hanging from a leather cord around my neck.

"I'm not sure," I said. I squirmed a bit. My necklace was short, so Coral had to lean in close to look. "My brother says it's fake. But I like it anyway."

"It's so cool," Coral said. "Is it supposed to be from a mako? It looks like it. Everyone loves great whites. But I think makos are *really* the best."

"Same," I said. I looked at Coral, amazed. I didn't know many other girls who were into shark facts.

"Did you know that makos . . ." Coral began.

". . . *are the fastest!*" We said it at the same time. Then we giggled.

"SHARED BRAIN!" Coral boomed. She rippled her fingers back and forth in the air, like invisible mind waves floating between our heads. I smiled back, but I looked around to see if anyone was watching. Coral's loud voice and wiggly fingers looked a bit dorky.

"I *really* couldn't believe it when I saw that the art theme was 'the sea,'" Coral said. "Art and the ocean are only, like, *the two best things ever.*"

I nodded. It was like we thought the same way. I wanted to be either an author or a marine biologist when I grew up. It's why I'd begged my parents to send me to this camp. At first they said it cost too much, but my nana offered to pay for half as an early birthday present. My whole family could see how much I wanted to go.

"Are you in Group B?" Coral asked me. When I answered yes, she jumped in the air and fist-pumped. I smiled, but inside I was wincing at Coral's energy burst.

"Hey, I want to show you something." Coral dropped her backpack onto the grass and pulled out a sketchbook. I watched as she flipped through page after page of cartoonish creatures. The drawings were rough and rushed — but there sure were plenty of them. I caught sight of dragons, wizards, robots and lots of hybrid human-fish creatures. All the heads seemed a bit too big for the bodies, and the legs looked short and squished. But I could tell that Coral had the kind of imagination that never stopped.

She shoved the book into my hands. "Look,"

she said, pointing to the open page. On it was a comic book style character. The bottom half of her body was a curvy mermaid tail covered in scales. On top, she was a tough-looking, teenage girl wearing a leather vest covered in zippers and studs. Her hair was big and curly, kind of like Coral's, only more seaweedy. The character's arms were bent in front of her, like she was flexing her muscles. Underneath it said, *Crash, the Mighty Mermaid Warrior*.

"Did you make her up?"

"Yup," Coral replied proudly. "I made her up last night! Wouldn't she make a great character in a comic book or graphic novel?"

"Uh-huh. I like her name too," I said.

"Crash — like a powerful wave slamming against the shore!" Coral bumped the side of her body into mine. I almost fell over.

"You know," I said, getting back my balance, "I started writing a story about a mermaid hero once."

"Really?" Coral's eyes went wide. "I told you we share a brain!"

"She's a bit . . . different from your character," I said. I looked at Crash's leather vest and flexed muscles. "She's powerful, but not like this. She's more like a secret spy."

"Tell me about her," Coral urged as she plopped down on the grass.

"Well . . ." I bit my lip and slowly sat down beside her. I didn't like telling people about my stories, at least not until they're finished and perfect. I had four top secret notebooks at home filled with stories that no one but me had seen. But there was something about Coral's big, friendly grin that made me feel I could trust her. Plus, telling someone about an idea isn't the same as giving them your words to read. You can always stop talking if the person looked bored.

"Okay," I said and took a deep breath. "My character's name is Driftwood. She's not like mermaids in other stories."

"Neither is Crash," said Coral.

"Right. Driftwood isn't always combing her hair and playing a harp."

Coral grabbed her throat and gagged. She clearly knew what I meant.

"Driftwood goes on secret missions throughout the ocean," I said.

"What kind of missions?" Coral asked.

"Mostly to protect the sea. Sometimes she rescues dolphins from fishing nets. Or she pushes polluting boats back toward the shore so they don't poison the water. Things like that."

Coral nodded, so I went on.

"I was even thinking that maybe Driftwood used to be a human. Maybe she was a lifeguard at the beach, good at protecting people. Then, one day, she gets turned into a mermaid hero. I'm not sure how it happens. But once she's a mermaid, she sees that the ocean needs protection as much as humans do. She finds it's her destiny to help."

I stopped when I noticed that Coral's mouth was hanging open, like a goldfish ready for food. Was she already bored? Did she hate my idea?

"Or . . . something like that," I mumbled. My cheeks felt warm. Maybe I shouldn't have

DYLAN'S FIRST DAY AS A LIFEGUARD

said anything. The story wasn't perfect. It wasn't even finished.

But Coral said, "That . . . is . . . *really* awesome! You're a great writer, Dylan. I can tell."

"You can?" I said, smiling.

"Oh!" Coral said springing onto her knees. She grabbed my wrists. She leaned her face close to mine.

"Why don't we be partners for the comic book workshop? We could put our characters together in the same story."

"They could form a Mermaid Warrior Squad!"

I knew about the comic book workshop and was looking forward to the story writing part. The drawing part made me a bit nervous. But I could see that drawing didn't scare Coral one bit.

"I can do most of the art since I love to draw," Coral continued, reading my mind. "And we could use your story. You have *amazing* ideas."

My face felt warm again, but in a good way. "I'd love to be partners with you," I said.

Coral fist-pumped, then said, "I wonder how our girls would meet?"

I thought about it until an idea bubbled to the surface. "Maybe at the beach?" I began. "It could be their first day as lifeguards. They meet each other and start working together. They see right away that they make a great team . . ."

"JUST LIKE US!" Coral boomed.

As Coral and I shared more ideas, I pictured our comic book coming to life. I could already see the panels, speech bubbles and perfect drawings, the kind you find in comics or graphic novels at the library. Who knew — maybe I'd learn to write like a real comic book writer. And Coral would learn to draw like a real artist.

Wasn't that the point of coming to this camp?

2
BRAIN WAVES

Art camp was two weeks long. Every day we had different workshops and activities. Kelsey announced that our very first workshop was going to be comic books. Coral and I couldn't believe our luck!

"Here," Coral said, dashing into the art room. I followed her to the table where she sat down to work. A girl whose nametag said *Lynn* was already there. She gave Coral and me a shy, tiny smile. She had glasses with purple frames and the straightest, shiniest black hair I'd ever seen, with thick bangs cut straight across.

"Let's jump right in and look at some sea

ART UNDER THE SEA!
SUMMER YOUTH ARTS CAMP

WORKSHOP SCHEDULE FOR
GROUP B: WEEK ONE

COMIC BOOKS	RECYCLED ART	COMIC BOOKS	RECYCLED ART	COMIC BOOKS
BREAK	BREAK	BREAK	BREAK	BREAK
MUSIC	FILM	MUSIC	FILM	MUSIC
LUNCH	LUNCH	LUNCH	LUNCH	LUNCH
GROUP GAMES	DRAMA	DANCE	DRAMA	DANCE
BREAK	BREAK	BREAK	BREAK	BREAK
DANCE	GROUP GAMES	SWIMMING	GROUP GAMES	THEATRE TOUR & SIGN UP FOR SHOWCASE

creatures," said our comic book instructor, Raina. She showed us photos of tropical fish, sharks and squids on a whiteboard hooked up to her tablet. We all talked about their body shapes and features.

"How about this guy?" Raina showed us the next picture. Everyone burst out laughing.

"Freaky!" someone said.

"What *is* that thing?" asked someone else.

I knew we were all looking at an elephant seal. I'd read about them in my shark books. Some sharks liked to eat them.

"I know!" Coral piped up. "It's a male elephant seal. You can tell because only the males have those trunk-shaped noses." That's what everyone was laughing at — the short, flabby trunk that curled from its face.

"They make this crazy honking noise too," Coral went on. "Like this . . ."

Oh no, I thought. *Coral isn't going to do it, is she?*

Coral opened her mouth and let out a sound like a lion's roar and a giant burp mashed together! It was funny, but it made everyone turn to stare in our direction. I wanted to shrink down into my T-shirt and hide.

"That . . . was . . . *awesome*," said Lamar, a boy at the next table. That gave Coral a reason to do it again! I noticed a couple of trendy girls across the room rolling their eyes and laughing. I wished I could slide under the table.

"Thanks for the lesson, Coral," said Raina with a grin.

Coral bowed forward in her seat. Lamar and his friend Ryan cheered.

"Okay — how about we start drawing?" Raina asked.

Yes, please! I thought.

Raina began to sketch on her tablet. We could see what she was drawing up on her whiteboard. Using just a few curvy strokes, Raina drew the outline of a blue whale. She told us to follow along.

We bent over our papers and copied Raina's shape. I was barely halfway through when I looked over. Coral was finished her messy whale sketch. She pushed her paper aside and opened the sketchbook she'd brought with her. "I'm going to start on Driftwood," she whispered. "I think she should be a ninja. Is that okay?" Coral asked.

"Sure," I said. As soon as Coral said it, I could picture Driftwood that way. Her talents were hiding and sneaking. Coral worked quickly. She gave Driftwood a mermaid tail and a sleek top, like she was wearing a dark bodysuit. She added a hood that covered her head and some of her face. Coral gave her a ponytail, like mine, and made it stick out from the hood at the back.

"What are those things hanging from their bracelets?" I asked as I looked at Crash and Driftwood's wrists.

"They're messaging devices," Coral said. "Crash and Driftwood can talk to each other through them if they ever get separated."

"Hey!" I said. "Like their lifeguard walkie-talkies, right?" I could perfectly picture the comic book panel where they turned from lifeguards to mermaids.

"Love it!" said Coral. She continued to make

lightning-fast drawings. Her sketches didn't look much like they did in my mind. But then again, it was only the first day of camp.

Later in the class, Raina gave us ideas for turning our animals into fantasy characters. "How about fairy wings on an octopus?" she said. With a few strokes, Raina turned an octopus into a magical, flying creature. Next, she put a pair of muscly human arms on her whale. I tried to do the same on my whale, but it ended up looking like he had a pair of cheese puffs growing out of his body. I had to erase so often, my hand got a cramp.

I took a break and looked around the room. Nearby, Lamar and Ryan were laughing their heads off. They were drawing a great white shark attacking a seal.

"Make his mouth more like this." Lamar stuck out his neck, rolled back his eyes and opened his mouth as wide as it could go.

"Lookin' good, dude," said Ryan.

Lamar punched Ryan in the arm.

Across the room, the trendy girls were

goofing around with the tall boy who sat behind them. He was poking the girl who had the long, dark, curly hair with the eraser end of his pencil.

"Stop it!" I heard her say. But I could tell she didn't mind at all. She leaned her head toward her friend with the straight dark hair. They started giggling. They both had matching bags that said *Diamond Dance Academy* in fancy writing. The girl with the curls had the word "SASSY" spelled out on hers in blingy gemstone letters.

A few minutes later, Raina told us to choose our favourite sea creature sketch and imagine it as a comic book character. We were supposed to think about its personality, its problems and its powers. We were allowed to work in partners, so Coral and I talked some more about our Crash and Driftwood characters.

"They should have an origin story," I said.

"What's that?" Coral said.

"It's a story about how the Mermaid Warriors got their powers in the first place," I said. "Lots of stories have them. Especially

SOMEONE NEEDS HELP.

THE OCEAN IS UNDER ATTACK BY PEOPLE WHO POLLUTE THE WATER. WE NEED MERMAID WARRIORS TO HELP US PROTECT THE SEA!

BUT BEFORE YOU DECIDE . . . SOMEONE STOLE THE BACK-TO-HUMAN-BALM. YOU'LL HAVE TO STAY MERMAIDS.

MAGIC MERMAID MORPHING LOTION

LET'S DO IT.

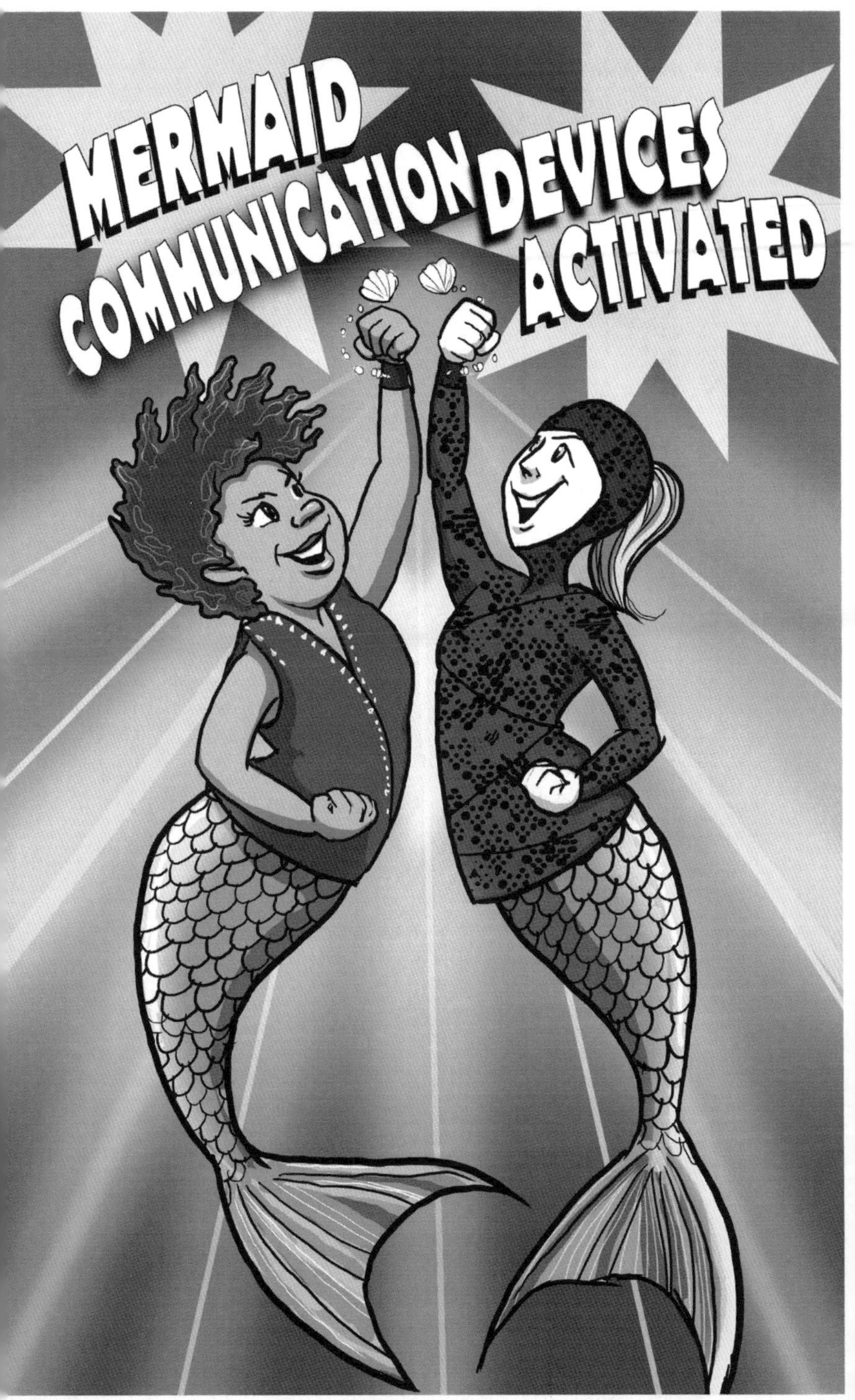
MERMAID COMMUNICATION DEVICES ACTIVATED

comic book stories." I'd learned about origin stories in creative writing from my grade five teacher, Ms. B.

"We know that our girls meet lifeguarding. Now we have to figure out how they transform," I said.

"Right."

"What if one day they see a person lying on the beach? She's partly in the water and partly on the sand. She looks hurt, so they go to check it out." I could hear my voice rising as my idea grew. "When they get there, they realize why she's partly in the water . . ."

"Ooo . . . I know!" Coral's eyes grew wide. "She's a mermaid, right? Maybe she's a magic mermaid who turns *them* into mermaids. But how? Does she just zap them, like an electric eel?"

I shook my head. "I don't think they should just get zapped. I think they have to make a choice about it." I had learned in creative writing that in the best stories, the hero has to make a tough choice.

"Can I use this page?" I asked. Coral pushed her sketchbook toward me. I drew little lines bursting out from her sketches of Crash and Driftwood. At the end of each line, I wrote words like *lifeguards*, *beach*, *magic mermaid* and *big choice* to help us remember our ideas. Coral and I kept coming up with words for our characters, each word sparking another. Eventually, it looked like Crash and Driftwood were caught in a fishing net of words.

I could tell that our voices were getting loud, especially Coral's. I looked to make sure no one was staring at us. Not everyone was planning their characters in the same way. Lamar and Ryan were adding crazy cartoon details to their sketches. At our table, Lynn had divided her paper into four straight-lined boxes. In them, she wrote neat lists under headings like PERSONALITY, GOALS, ACTIVITIES and FRIENDS. Meanwhile, the dancer diva girls were taking turns making squishy-lipped model faces and drawing each other.

"This is going to be EPIC!" Coral said.

She slammed her fist on our table so hard, Lynn's pencil jumped right out of her hand. Lamar and Ryan turned to look. I noticed the diva dancers laughing at us again from across the room.

I ducked my head. I agreed with Coral. I could picture our characters transforming into Crash and Driftwood.

But did Coral have to shout about it?

3
THROUGH DEEP AND SHALLOW

"Hey, Lynn!" Coral called out. Coral and I were sitting on the lawn eating our lunch and talking about ideas for our comic book. "I made you part of the Mermaid Warrior Squad!"

On a scrap of paper, Coral had drawn a hybrid dolphin-girl creature (although I thought it looked more like a duck than a dolphin). You could tell it was supposed to look like Lynn, with its thick black bangs and glasses. Coral wanted to turn everyone in our group into characters in our comic book. But I didn't think we were ready to share, at least for now.

Lynn took the drawing from Coral. "It's cute. Thanks." She tucked Dolphin/Duck Girl into her mini backpack.

"Lamar and Ryan get to be Shark Dudes," Coral announced getting ready to draw some more.

Just then, Kelsey's voice blasted through the megaphone she carried when we were outside. "Group B — time for games! Boys to me. Girls by the tree," she said.

Coral, Lynn and I headed for the tree with the other girls. Lynn and I walked normally. Coral skipped and hopped and skittered around, like she'd eaten too much sugar. That's when I noticed the trendy girls scoffing at us nearby. The "SASSY" one with the long, curly hair pointed in our direction. She put her hand in front of her mouth and said something to her friend. They burst out laughing, and my stomach flip-flopped.

"Coral," I whispered. "Stop jumping around. Those girls are looking."

"Who, them?" Coral asked, pointing right

at the divas. "Hi, Sarina!" Coral called out and waved. "I know one of them from school," she explained.

"Coral — *shh*," I said.

As Coral moved closer to the girls, I shuffled slowly after her.

"I didn't know you were coming to this camp, Sarina," Coral said. "What's so funny, anyway?"

"Oh . . . nothing," said the girl with the straight hair. She bit her lip and shook her head, like she really didn't want to say. She glanced over at the "SASSY" girl. This time I was close enough to see that her nametag said *Jade*.

"Come on," Coral insisted. "You're laughing at something."

"Oh, fine," said Jade. She crossed her arms in front of her. She smiled like a mako shark while Sarina looked down at her shoes. "I was just wondering why anyone would do their hair that way. That's all."

I thought at first that Jade was teasing Coral for not being a long-haired, girly diva like they were. But then I noticed where Jade's eyes were pointed — at me! Jade smiled and twisted one of her curls around her finger.

"What way?" I said. My voice barely came out as a whisper.

"You know, shaved like that — when you could just have nice, normal, long hair." Jade's sugary voice didn't match the garbage-face she was making.

My hands flew up to touch my hair. My cousin had given me an edgy new cut for camp. She'd buzzed the sides and all the way underneath, leaving the top hair long enough for a ponytail. When I first got my haircut, I'd loved it. Now, all I could think of was yanking out my ponytail and pulling the long parts down over the buzzed bits!

"I *really* like Dylan's hair," said Coral, stepping forward. "It's different."

Jade narrowed her eyes at Coral. "That's funny coming from *you*, T-shirt Twins." Beside her, Sarina giggled. It made me want to melt into the grass.

"Everyone at camp got this shirt," said Coral.

"I know." Jade wrinkled her nose. "I gave mine to my brother."

Coral threw her arm around my shoulder. "Well, *we* think they're cool, right, Dylan?" she said.

"Girls, we're about to start," Kelsey called through her megaphone. "Can you move even closer to the tree?"

Coral skipped toward the tree like everything was fine. I dragged myself along after her.

Suddenly, a boy shot out from behind the tree and grabbed Jade by the shoulders. She shrieked as loud as a gym teacher's whistle.

"GOTCHA!" It was the tall boy. His nametag said *Ben*.

Jade's screams turned into squealy giggles. "You're *so* immature," she said, smiling like she'd just won a prize.

"You should have seen your face!" Ben laughed. "I wish I had recorded it." He lunged forward and grabbed Jade's arm.

She pulled away with another shriek. "Cut

it out," she giggled, as Ben started to chase her around.

Coral poked me in the ribs with her elbow. "And they think *we're* weirdos!" she said rolling her eyes. I didn't care what Jade was doing, as long as it wasn't staring at us and making fun!

But then, suddenly, Ben's eyes were on me.

"Hey — isn't Dylan a boy's name?" he said pointing to my nametag.

Why was the whole world judging me? First my hair, then my clothes . . . now even my *name*? My eyes began to feel hot and wet. I couldn't stop it.

"Dylan can be anyone's name," Coral said sticking out her chin.

"I wasn't talking to *you*," said Ben. He made a garbage-face just like Jade's.

"Dylan doesn't talk unless her *really* cool 'twin' talks for her," said Jade. She and Ben laughed at us, then continued their dumb chase.

I knew if I stood there any longer tears would spill out.

"I . . . have to . . . *bathroom* . . ." I barely got the word out to Coral before I took off.

"Dylan — wait!" Coral yelled.

"Found some," Coral said. She came out of a stall and handed me a few sheets of toilet paper.

"Thanks," I said taking the paper and dabbing my eyes.

"I don't know that Jade girl," Coral said. "She must be Sarina's friend from dancing. But Sarina's not always like that. She was in my class last year. We did science projects together."

I tried to picture Coral and that dancing diva working together. I couldn't see it.

"Sometimes when Sarina's around some people, she acts all snooty and says dumb stuff. But it doesn't mean anything."

I shrugged. I knew that Coral was trying to cheer me up. But hearing that Sarina could be a nice person didn't change the fact that she stuck with Jade.

"Hey — watch this!" said Coral. She put a hand on one of her hips and pranced back and forth in front of the sinks. She swung her hips from side to side like a model on a fashion runway. She even went up on her tiptoes, like she was wearing high heels.

"I'm SO fantastic!" Coral said. She blew duck-face kisses at the mirror and fluffed up her hair with her hand. Then she said, "Whoa!" as she wobbled from side to side. She swooped her arms in circles and then made herself tumble to the bathroom floor. I couldn't help but laugh.

Coral smiled. "See? What's the point of being all like that?"

I shook my head. I knew what she meant. She and I definitely weren't the "sassy" type.

"We're the Comic Book Girls," Coral went on as she got up. "Plus, we know more about sharks than anyone else!"

That's why everyone thinks we're dorks, I thought. But I didn't say it out loud.

"And . . . we also know something about elephant seals," Coral added with a grin.

Then she sucked in a big breath and did her famous burp-roar. The echo off the bathroom walls made it ten times louder. Coral roared a few more times, even louder. Soon we were both laughing our heads off.

I even gave the roar a try myself. Just not as big.

4
GO WITH THE FLOW

The next day, our group had drama with an instructor named Morgan. We sat on the floor while Morgan told us about some of the plays he'd been in. Then he asked if we had any questions.

"Have you ever been in a movie?" said Jade.

"No," said Morgan.

"What about a TV show?" asked Sarina. "Even just a commercial?"

"Nope and nope," said Morgan.

"Why not?" Jade asked.

"I prefer live theatre. That's why I went into acting. For me, there's nothing like the feeling of acting on stage in front of people. Anything can happen!"

"Do you ever do pranks on each other?" said Ben.

Coral poked me and rolled her eyes. Ben was obsessed with pranks! In the film workshop that morning, Ben had bragged that he knew a group of "real" filmmakers. It turned out he was talking about his older brother Chase and his friends. They posted videos they made of themselves playing tricks on people at their school. Ben thought Chase's prank videos were hilarious.

"Pranks?" Morgan asked.

"Like, do you ever booby trap the props and stuff? To see if you can mess the other actors up," said Ben.

"Ah," said Morgan. He stroked his bushy beard. "Sometimes actors play good-natured tricks on each other. But I wouldn't recommend it. Pranks have a way of backfiring."

Ben waved his hand around, probably to ask more questions about pranks. But Morgan pretended not to see.

"Time to act!" Morgan said, clapping his hands. "We're going to warm up with an improv game. The trick is . . . there's no script for the actors."

No script? I felt my nerves wiggle like electric eels.

"I'm going to ask you to imagine a place. Then, acting together, you have to convince us that you're in that place. First, I need three volunteers . . ." Morgan's eyes swooped over our group, like a searchlight looking for escaped prisoners. I clenched my teeth and held my breath. Coral was already fidgeting and waving her hand around in the air. A few others in our group were doing the same, like they couldn't wait to get up there and embarrass themselves.

I hugged my knees close to my body. I made myself into a tiny ball. I was glad I had worn my hair down. When I tilted my head it made a curtain for my face, protecting me from Morgan's notice.

"How about . . . Lamar," Morgan called out. "And Jade . . ."

Out of the corner of my eye, I could see Coral swooping her arm back and forth, like she was directing an airplane to the landing strip. Then I felt her tug at my arm, trying to get me to raise my hand, too. *No!* I pressed my elbows tightly to my ribs. *Please, not me. Not yet!* I thought.

"And . . . Coral!" Morgan said.

Coral bounded from her spot to join Lamar and Jade. I finally let out my breath and relaxed my body. Morgan had his three volunteers. I was safe.

Morgan explained a few rules for the game. The first improv rule was, "Don't say 'no,' just go with the flow!" Basically, it meant that if Jade said, "Hey, everyone — let's be ballet dancers!" Lamar and Coral would have to twirl around with her.

"Ready? You are having a day at the aquarium. One . . . two . . . three, go!"

For a moment, no one did a thing. There was an awkward silence, and some of the audience giggled. Coral was as still as a statue. She'd been so excited to get up there, but now she couldn't think of anything to do. I felt bad for her. It was exactly why I could never go first.

Suddenly, Lamar started walking back and forth in front of us. He made a fist and brought it near his mouth, like he was holding a microphone. "We'll be feeding the sharks in five minutes," he said in a deep voice, like he was a tour guide. "Hurry to get a good view of the feeding frenzy." We all laughed at Lamar's funny voice.

Next, Coral began to move. She dropped to her knees and leaned forward. She put one of her hands behind her head, fingers pointing straight up, to make a shark's dorsal fin. Then she wiggled her body back and forth and pretended to swim.

Jade strolled by. She had her right elbow bent, like she was holding somebody's arm. She stopped and looked at Coral.

Jade turned to her invisible date. "Oh, sweetie, thanks for taking me to the aquarium," she said. "I love seeing all the *adorable* little fishies!" She batted her eyelashes and everyone laughed.

Then Jade pointed at Coral and gasped. "Ew! What a weird-looking elephant seal. Is that really its face?" The group laughed again. We all thought of the crazy picture Raina had shown us. I wasn't sure if Jade was calling Coral weird-looking on purpose. If that were me up there, I would have died!

But not Coral — she came to *life*. "Arr! Arr! Arr!" she barked. Just like that, Coral morphed from shark into seal. She tucked her elbows tight to her sides and flapped her hands around like flippers. She honked like a seal. She shuffle-walked around in her tank, as though she had flippers instead of legs.

"Ick," said Jade. "I don't want to see the yucky animals with the weird faces. I want to see the *cute* fishies." She tossed her hair and started to walk away.

"ARR-rawwwwww!" Coral bellowed. She lifted her arm and curled it in front of her head like it was a flabby elephant seal trunk.

"Oh no — she's getting upset," shouted Lamar. "You don't want to see her upset!"

And then Coral took things to a whole new level.

First, she started flopping her head around. It really did look like she was bumping it against the glass.

Lamar caught on to what Coral was pretending to do. He started calling out sound effects: "BOOOOOM! CRRRRRACK! SMAAAASH!"

It was amazing. We all could see Coral the elephant seal smash her way out of her tank!

"Arr! Arr! Arr!" With a frantic bark, Coral "escaped" through the broken glass wall. Lamar shrieked and tossed his invisible microphone into the air. "I quit!" he shouted, and pretended to run away. But Coral the Seal wasn't after him. She was flapping her flippers and waddling after Jade. Jade tried to skitter away — for real!

Coral caught up to Jade, who had nowhere to turn. Coral leaned forward and nudged Jade's shoulder with her head. "Arr! Cute . . . fishy . . . Arr!" Coral said, in a cartoonish seal voice.

By this time, our group was falling over with laughter.

"Why are you touching me?" Jade hissed at Coral. But Coral kept on butting Jade with her head. She was having a blast.

"And . . . FREEZE," Morgan said. "Great job you three! You aren't professional improv actors, are you?"

Lamar and Coral both took a bow as our group clapped. Coral went down on one knee and threw her arms out to her sides, like she wanted to hug us all. Meanwhile Jade's lips were pressed tight together. It looked like she was hiding a mouth full of clenched teeth. She marched back to her spot beside Sarina and crossed her arms as she sat down.

Coral scooched into her place beside me.

"Great job," I said.

"Thanks! You should go next," she said.

For half a second, I thought about putting up my hand. A million acting ideas had sparked in my mind: A nervous aquarium worker feeding a starving shark . . . A little kid throwing a tantrum because he dropped his ice cream into the tank . . . A beluga whale who thinks he's the one on tour, watching the humans on the other side of the glass . . .

But I turned to Coral and whispered, "*No way.*"

I knew that in front of the group, my mind would be blank. With everyone watching, my body would freeze.

5
CHOPPY WATERS

"I think the Mermaid Warrior Squad needs villains," I said to Coral. We were holding on to flutter boards and kicking around in the water. Our group was swimming in the big outdoor pool near the college.

I swam over to the side of the pool and ditched my board. Coral did the same. We clung to the ledge and faced each other.

"Okay, let's think," Coral said. Then she switched to her tough Crash voice. "Come on, Driftwood! Mermaid Warriors think better when they swim."

She pushed off from the wall and plunged

headfirst under the water. Her feet broke the surface as she tried a handstand. Her legs soon slumped to one side as her crooked handstand collapsed. She popped up to catch a quick breath.

"Come on!" Coral said between gasps. We did a few handstands, then some cartwheels, then a few backward flips. I peeked a few times to see if anyone was watching us, then dove back under the water. I loved the quiet under the surface. The blue and white tiles at the bottom of the pool were lit up by sunbeams. As we swam through streams of light, I imagined glowing energy beams giving the Mermaid Warriors extra powers . . .

When we were tired of swimming, Coral and I found inner tubes to float on. I dipped under the water and shot myself up through the donut hole of my floater so I could hang over its edge. Coral hiked herself up onto the top of hers. Her wet skin squeaked on the rubber as she wiggled her backside into the hole. When she was in, she lay back like a movie star in a lounge chair.

"Should the enemies be fantasy sea creatures?" Coral asked. She loved drawing monsters and weird looking hybrid fish-people. She chopped the water with a few warrior punches and a loud warrior grunt. "Or should they be like the human polluters in your original Driftwood story? Or maybe they could . . ."

Suddenly, Coral's tube flipped right over. She was dumped under water with a huge splash!

"Coral!" I called out. I started kicking my way over to where she'd vanished. That's when I spotted Ben's laughing head sticking out of the water nearby.

"Did you just . . ." I said to him. Hands yanked on my ankles below the water. ". . . Hey!" I felt a strong tug. The next thing I knew, I went down through the donut hole!

I kicked my legs free from the grabbing hands and flipped myself around. I surfaced in time to see Jade and Sarina dangling from my tube. Jade's eyes were twinkling as I swam to Coral, who had popped up from the water coughing and spluttering.

"Nice moves, mermaids!" Ben chuckled. His body bobbed up and down in the tube that had belonged to Coral.

Jade and Sarina laughed. They followed Ben as he paddled away.

"THOSE ARE OUR FLOATERS!" shouted Coral. "Hey, Dylan — let's get Lamar and Ryan to help us. We should go after those dunkers!" Her eyes were wide and bright, like she was having fun.

"WATER WAR!" Coral bellowed. "JUSSSSS-TICE!" She was about to plow into the water and go after them. But I held her arm to stop her. Dozens of people were already staring at us. And what if the lifeguard kicked us out of the pool — in front of everyone?

"Forget it, Coral — please. Can't we just sit on the stairs and talk about our story?" I steered Coral toward the steps leading down into the pool. At least there no one could grab us by surprise.

"Okay," Coral said. "But I don't think we'll have any problems thinking up enemies now.

How about three pirates named Ben, Jade and Sarina!"

I narrowed my eyes in the direction of the dunkers. They were swimming up to a bunch of kids playing water volleyball and looked ready for another ambush.

"I think we could make up more interesting villains than that," I said, watching the pranksters in action.

Coral scrunched up her lips. "You're right. They'd be totally boring to draw. Oo! I drew this cool hammerhead-octopus hybrid guy once — a hammer-pus. What about him?"

I closed my eyes and tried to imagine something more sinister than a "hammer-pus." My mind became an underwater camera, dropping down, down, down. It went deep into the ocean where it was dark and mysterious, deeper than any shark would ever go. Near the ocean floor, it was cold and silent. There were strange fish living there. They had scaly bodies that glowed dimly like old light bulbs. Long strands of seaweed rippled like wavy hair.

But wait! Seaweed doesn't grow this deep! What under-the-sea could those rippling strands be?

My eyes flew open. "I've got something," I said. "What if the enemies are seaweed creatures? They hide out at the bottom of the ocean, like underwater ghosts!"

"Ooo . . . I like that," Coral said, her eyes wide. "They would be super sneaky. Maybe they camouflage themselves as sea plants when they leave their hideout. That's how they spy on the Mermaid Warriors and then . . . *attack*!"

"Yes!" I said. "And how about this? *They used to be mermaids.* Maybe even Mermaid Warriors." I thought of the seaweed strands I'd seen in my mind rippling like long mermaid hair. "But they turned bad somehow . . ."

". . . and became the Seaweed Sisters!" Coral shouted. She slammed the water with her fist.

"Seaweed Sisters . . . that's perfect," I said. I loved how both words began with a slithery sounding "s."

"But why do they go after the Mermaid Warriors?" Coral asked.

I pressed my lips together, then said, "Well, in my story, Driftwood fought bad humans who were polluting the ocean . . ."

"I liked that," said Coral. "So, should we just forget about the Seaweed Sisters then?"

"I didn't mean forget about them," I said. Coral was always so quick to leap from one idea to the next. "I was just thinking of a way to combine the two ideas . . ." I felt the flash of an idea. "What if the Seaweed Sisters are *helping* one of the bad humans?"

"But why would they do that?" Coral asked. "Don't they live in the sea too?"

"Maybe they like living in toxic waste. It gives them more power or something . . ."

"Oh, that's good!" Coral blurted.

"And the polluter guy promises the Sisters power. Once he rules the sea, they will too."

"Whoa!" Coral said. "So — what's this human polluter guy going to be like?"

We were interrupted by a yell and splash.

We both looked in the direction of the noise. Ben had just flipped Lamar and Ryan off of the blow-up raft they'd been floating on. Ben swam away with a mean grin on his face.

"Let's call him Captain Fishhead," I said.

CAPTAIN FISHHEAD IS USING THE SEA AS HIS DUMPING GROUND.

6
SHARING TREASURE

Coral and I were working together in the recycled art room. Our job was to turn art supplies and junk into things that looked like they belonged in the sea. The art pieces were going to be used as props in the skits for the special showcase at the end of camp. I was still making an underwater sea plant out of green bendy straws and clay, just like one of the sample creations we were given as models at the first workshop. Meanwhile, Coral kept coming back to our table with armloads of colourful materials. She didn't follow a plan. She just lumped stuff together until it started to look like something from the ocean.

"This one's going to be a jellyfish," Coral said. It was her third ocean creature puppet. She held up an old margarine container that she'd covered in a shiny, whitish-pinkish wrapping paper. "I'm going to bring some streamers from home to make the tentacles. I *actually* have tons in the craft room in my basement."

"You have a craft room?" I asked. I didn't even have a basement at my house, never mind an extra room just for crafts. We had our bedrooms, a kitchen, a living room and that's it (plus a bathroom, of course).

"Hey, I almost forgot," said Coral. "I made this for you." She reached into her pocket and pulled out a bright green loop bracelet. Every loop in the bracelet was tucked into the next one, making a row of Vs, almost like a real fishtail. Dangling from it was a round metal disk about the size of a loonie. Coral had printed "MWS" on the disk with a gold marker. The letters stood for Mermaid Warrior Squad, of course.

"Look — I have the same one." Coral thrust out her wrist, showing me her identical bracelet.

"Thanks," I said. I slipped the rubber circle over my wrist. "Are these little medals from your craft room too?"

"Yeah. I have a whole box full."

I was impressed. Coral's craft room must be like a craft store!

"Don't you think they're like Crash and Driftwood's messaging bracelets?" Coral asked.

"They're nice," I said.

"I've been making loop bracelets forever," said Coral. "Actually — *weird!* — I think Sarina was the one who showed me how."

I looked across the room at Sarina. She was making a giant starfish out of wire hangers and cloth. Beside her, Jade laughed as Ben flicked water toward Lynn's head with a paintbrush. In his other hand, Ben held a digital camera and filmed his mean little gag.

Ben, Ryan and some of the other campers had signed up to make a documentary. It was going to be posted on the camp website when camp was over. They got to carry around cameras and film interesting moments at camp. Ryan had even interviewed Coral and me about our comic book. But Ben only turned on his camera when he was playing a joke on someone, or when he spotted something embarrassing.

"Crash to Driftwood. Come in, Driftwood," I heard Coral say. She was talking into her bracelet to get my attention. She laughed when I looked her way. "Hey — why don't I show you how to make these at lunch? They're pretty easy after your first two or three."

"I know how already," I said. I didn't add that I'd known how since grade three.

"Perfect!" said Coral. "Then we'll be able to make a whole bunch to give away! At home, I have enough MWS medallions for everyone!"

"Everyone?" I asked. "I thought these were like the messaging bracelets in our story. Just for us."

"We can add extra things to ours to make

them different. I have some plastic fish charms at home," Coral said. "Don't you want everyone at camp to remember the Comic Book Girls?"

How could I make Coral understand? I liked telling my ideas to her and watching her turn them into drawings. It was fun. But our comic book wasn't ready to share with the world. Why couldn't we keep it private until it was good enough?

"Are we going to make bracelets for them, too?" I nodded my head in the direction of our real-life villains.

"Why not? Maybe they'll be nicer to us if we give them something cool."

Somehow, I couldn't imagine Jade, Sarina and Ben thinking our bracelets were cool.

"Come on," Coral grabbed my arm. "Let's go ask Lamar and Ryan if they'll wear them."

I put down my green straws and clay and followed Coral. Lamar and Ryan were hunched over their large papier mâché creature. It was starting to come to life. You could already tell from the open mouth and the pointy dorsal fin that it was going to be a great white. It looked really good. Lamar and Ryan called their shark Bob.

"Dylan and I are going to make these for everyone in our group," Coral said. She grabbed my wrist so we could both show Ryan and Lamar our bracelets. "Would you guys wear them around at camp?"

"Sure," said Ryan, looking at the bracelets.

"What are those dangly thingies?" Lamar asked.

"That's the official Mermaid Warrior Squad emblem," said Coral. "If anyone asks you what MWS stands for, you can tell them. And tell them that the Comic Book Girls made them." She gave me a wink.

"Can you do hockey colours?" Ryan asked. "I'd take a red and blue one."

"What about black and grey?" Lamar asked.

"I *actually* have a bunch of loops in my bag in every colour. And lots of these disks for our emblem." Coral winked again. "That's the important part."

"Wait! If you're making a whole bunch, can we have extra?" asked Lamar. He exchanged a look with Ryan.

"Oh ... *right*," Ryan said, catching on. "We'll take as many bracelets as you can give us!"

"We'll buy you smoothies from the cafeteria as our payment," promised Lamar.

"Okay," Coral instantly agreed. "We'll make you some at lunch. And more on our breaks."

I raised my eyebrows. "I thought we were going to use our breaks to work on our comic. Remember how we have to restart page three?" During our last comic book workshop, Coral forgot to leave room for words in two of the comic book panels.

"It's okay," said Coral. "We can do both things!"

I shook my head. *That's the problem!* I wanted to say. Coral was always doing too many things at once. In the end, nothing turned out quite right.

"What do you need so many bracelets for, anyway?" I asked the boys.

"Promise not to say?" Lamar asked Coral and me.

We promised.

"Okay," Ryan said in a hushed voice. "See Bob? He isn't just a great white shark."

Ryan had us lean in closer toward Bob. Then Lamar glanced around the room. When he was sure no one was watching, he removed a few loose pieces of tape at the base of the dorsal fin and lifted it off. Coral and I looked into the hole that Bob's fin had covered up and peered into the hollow shark body.

"He's going to be a great, big . . . *piñata*!" Lamar whispered.

"On the last day of camp, after the showcase, we're going to fill up Bob with candy and prizes. And things like your bracelets," Ryan explained.

"We'll seal it up with tissue paper and tape, so no one will know," said Lamar.

"And then at the big camp party . . . *wham-o*!" said Ryan. He slashed the air with an invisible stick.

"This is a *really* amazing idea," Coral said, admiring Bob. "We'll make as many bracelets as we can. Right, Dylan?"

I knew Coral was picturing thousands of MWS bracelets raining down from the sky for everyone at camp.

"Right," I mumbled.

I was starting to worry we'd never finish our comic!

7
THAT SINKING FEELING . . .

On Friday, our group had a tour of the building where the big showcase was going to take place. First, we saw a large room with tall walls and a high ceiling where our ocean art pieces would be displayed. Coral and I had already given Kelsey two of our favourite comic pages to put in a frame and hang on the wall. Besides the art display, there was also a going to be a variety show with skits and musical numbers. We all had to help out with the show in some way. Some people were performing, and Coral and I were going to create props and scenery.

"Wow," I said under my breath. The big theatre hall we went into next sloped down toward a stage with heavy blue curtains. There were rows and rows of plush grey seats, like you find in a fancy movie theatre.

"How many people can sit in here, do you think?" I asked Coral. We walked down the aisle with our group. "Two hundred?"

"More," she said. "Probably a thousand!"

Jade announced loud enough for everyone to hear: "This place looks like my school's auditorium."

"No *way* do you *really* have this kind of theatre at your school," said Coral.

Secretly, I agreed. What kind of school could have a room like this? When my school put on a concert or a play, it was in our gym. The audience sat in folding chairs, and the stage rolled away.

Jade gave Coral her classic garbage-face look.

"Yes, we *really* do, Coral," said Jade. "We put on amazing plays and musicals every year."

"Jade was the lead this year," Sarina said.

Of course, she was, I thought.

"We're going to go backstage now," Kelsey said, showing us the way.

We went through a door, then a hallway. We passed a dressing room and a place where props and costumes were stored.

Next, we came into a space just to the side of the stage itself. "This area is called the wing," Kelsey explained. "There's another wing just like it right across from us. This is where performers will make one last tweak to their costumes, and then . . ." Kelsey stepped right out onto the stage. ". . . *showtime!*"

We wandered onto the stage, looking this way and that. Everyone seemed just as impressed as I felt. Even Jade.

"WHOA," hollered Coral, stomping over to investigate every corner.

"This is so cool!" cried Lamar, taking a fake bow. He and Ryan started talking about their puppet show starring Bob the shark and the rest of their fish puppets. They called it "Predator Vs. Prey."

I stood still in the middle of the stage and stared out at the rows of seats. I wondered how loud I'd have to speak for someone to hear me all way at the back . . .

Coral tapped me on the shoulder. "Check it out," she said. I turned to see what she was looking at. The back wall of the stage was lit up with an underwater video like it was a giant movie screen.

"Neat," I said. We watched a school of shimmering fish swim by.

"That's so awesome!" said Ryan.

"My prank videos would look great up there," I heard Ben say.

"Do we *have* to have that screen on behind us when we perform?" Jade asked Kelsey in a whiny voice. She and Sarina were going to do a dance number to a pop song called "Tidal Wave Crush." She was probably worried that a video would distract the audience from looking at anything but her.

"The video background is optional, Jade," said Kelsey. "It depends on your performance.

Our backstage crew is just trying out a few things this afternoon."

"Do they have any shark attack videos?" asked Lamar. "Sharks hunting *animals*, I mean, not people. We could use it for 'Predator Vs. Prey'!"

I heard a sharp "Oo!" burst from Coral. On the screen, a big boat glided over the surface of the water. It cast a dark shadow on the underwater scene below. Coral stared up at it in silence. I wasn't sure why, and silence was a bit strange for Coral!

I shrugged and turned back to look out at the rows of seats. Suddenly, I could imagine what the theatre would look like on the night of a fancy show. The seats would be filled up with people wearing dressy clothes and holding programs. I pictured myself stepping into the spotlight as the underwater scene rippled behind me. I was dressed like a magic ocean queen in a gown of shimmering purple and silver. My hair flowed over my shoulders in long, rippling, dark curls. On my head, I wore a tall crown made of spiky orange coral . . .

"So are you thinking what I'm thinking?" Coral asked. We were leaving the theatre and walking back into the big display room.

"I don't know," I said. "Am I?" I blinked my eyes. I had looked right into one of the spotlights as we left the stage. "What are you thinking, Coral?"

"Didn't that underwater video make you think of our comic book?" she asked. "When the boat floated across the top of the screen? It made me think of Captain Fishhead!"

"I guess," I answered.

"And didn't it make you think that we could make it part of the show? 'Mermaid Warrior Squad: Live on Stage!'" Coral boomed.

"What?" I rubbed my eyes, trying to bring Coral into focus.

"We can make our comic into a skit for the showcase. It would be amazing!"

A skit? I thought. What was Coral talking

about? I wasn't going out on that stage . . . not for real . . . not in front of an audience!

"Group B — listen up," Kelsey called out to us. "I've got the sign up sheet for the showcase. Remember, if you aren't signing up to perform, you can put down your name to make props and costumes. There's something for everyone to do."

Lamar, Ryan, Jade and Sarina rushed toward Kelsey right away. They knew exactly what they were going to perform. Coral was about to run too, but I grabbed her arm.

"Wait," I said. "I thought we were going to sign up to make props."

"We've made lots of stuff already," said Coral. "This will be more fun!"

I shook my head. "But, I *like* making things, Coral."

"Don't worry, Dylan. I have the whole skit figured out," said Coral. She wasn't listening to me at all. "Picture it — I'll come out from one wing as Crash, and you'll come out from the other as Driftwood. We can have the backstage guys play that boat video. Maybe we'll have a narrator tell a bit of the story. Oo! And there could be music . . ."

My head was spinning. Coral made it sound like we'd already signed up. And her skit ideas didn't make any sense to me. Who was going to be the narrator? What were the Mermaid Warriors supposed to do battle with . . . the video screen? Everything Coral said crashed together in my brain and made a tangled mess.

"I thought finishing up our comic book was going to be our big project," I said.

Coral waved her hand through the air. "We can do both! Trust me, the skit won't take that long to write."

Not if you write it, I thought, knowing Coral's speedy way of doing everything. I thought of the often not-so-awesome results. If the two of us didn't take the time to make it good, I could just see how awkward we'd look up there.

Then, I didn't have to imagine it.

Right there — in front of everyone — Coral became Crash. She kicked the air and chopped invisible enemies. She threw punches to the left and right. She boomed out grunts and growls to match her moves.

"*Coral*," I whispered. "*Stop!*" Of course, she didn't. When did Coral ever care who was watching?

And everyone was watching. Jade and Sarina rolled their eyes and copied some of Coral's gestures. Even Ryan and Lamar were sending a funny look in our direction. And they were our friends.

Then I spotted Ben. He had his camera pointed straight at us! I jumped out of view and tried to drag Coral with me. But Coral wrenched herself free. When she saw the camera, it was like someone flipped her "on" switch.

"Hah! Ugh! *Rrrrrrrr*-aaaaah! MERMAID WARRIOR SQUAD!" she howled. She moved right up to the camera, giving Ben close-up views of her awkward punches and kicks, and her sweaty face.

I dashed away. It was the perfect time for a bathroom break.

8
SEA SICKNESS

"This is the kitchen," said Coral. "My bedroom is down the hall."

I was on a tour of Coral's house. It was Saturday and Coral had invited me to spend the afternoon at her place.

I poked my head into Coral's room. I saw a jumble of colourful objects piled high on Coral's desk and crammed onto every shelf. Most things were homemade, like a flock of slightly crushed origami birds, and a group of wobbly clay bowls. Coral's hand-sketched comic book creatures were tacked all over the walls. That room could only belong to Coral!

"Now — let's check out my craft room," said Coral. "There's something I *really* have to show you."

We walked back down the hall toward the basement stairs. "By the way, this is the bathroom." Coral pointed out a tiny room just before we reached the stairs. "You have to jiggle the handle on the toilet to get it to flush. But don't worry — it works." I peeked into the bathroom. It was even smaller than the one at my house.

I was surprised at how small Coral's house was, at least compared to what I'd imagined. From the way Coral talked about her "craft room", the "movie room" and all the fun activities she did at home, I had pictured a mansion. But her house wasn't much bigger than mine.

"Here we are," Coral said at the bottom of the stairs. We stood in a small basement, the kind with a concrete floor and the pipes showing in the ceiling.

"That's it!" She pointed to an area separated from the washing machine by a big piece of cardboard. It wasn't a craft room at all. It was just a long folding table, an old chair and some mismatched storage bins stuffed with craft supplies. It wasn't bad or anything, just not what I expected. But I could see Coral was very proud of it.

"Close your eyes," Coral said. So I did.

I heard her shuffling around by the table. Then she said, "You can look now."

Coral stood in front of me with a grin. Hanging from her waist and all the way down to her feet was a sort of green, plastic apron. The bottom flared out into two pointy shapes, like the end of a fishtail. She swung her hips from side to side to swish it around.

Oh no, I thought. I knew exactly what it was . . . and exactly what it was for.

"It's Crash's tail, for our skit. Isn't it great?" Coral said. "I made it last night. I cut it out of an old shower curtain. Isn't it *really* lucky that I had a green one?"

"Oh," I said. My voice was barely a squeak. *Lucky* wasn't the right word. More like *icky*.

"What's wrong?" Coral asked. But before I

could answer, she went on, "Oh, don't worry. I made one for you too."

My stomach sank.

After fumbling around on her table, Coral handed me my shower-curtain tail. It looked awful. I stood there holding my tail away from me like it was on fire.

"And check this out," Coral said. She grabbed a piece of shiny black plastic with two big holes in it. She stuck an arm through each of the holes. "Crash's leather vest," Coral explained. "I made it from a garbage bag. See these little foil bits I glued all over it? They're the metal studs."

I didn't say a word.

"I'll show you how to put your tail on," Coral offered. She grabbed the tail from my hands and looped the cloth "belt" around my waist. "We'll have to wear shorts or tights or something since the tail doesn't cover the back. But this way we can walk around and do all our battle moves on stage, and . . . Dylan? What's the matter?"

I felt my teeth grinding together. I didn't want to hurt Coral's feelings. That's why I'd let her sign us up to act in the showcase, even though the idea made my stomach hurt. But her junky costumes *stunk*! I didn't want to go out on stage in front of hundreds of people in the first place. And surely not dressed in *this*.

"Coral," I began. "I think it's cool that you tried to make our costumes."

"No problem!"

"But . . . remember what Kelsey said? We're going to be making props and costumes for the show all week. And the art teachers will be there to help us make everything look more . . . professional."

"I know. But why not make a few extra things?" said Coral. "I thought we could practise some moves, then work on the script and then . . ." She looked at my face and stopped talking. I must have looked as sea sick as I felt.

"What's wrong, Dylan?" Coral asked. "Don't you want to do this?"

This was my big chance to shout, "No, Coral. I *don't* want to do this!" But I didn't want to ruin our afternoon. Once, I had a fight with

HERE, LET ME HELP YOU.

NO, YOU GO ON AHEAD.

I NEED SOME QUIET TIME.

my best friend at school, and we didn't talk for a whole week. I felt sick the whole time.

Wait.

That was it!

I could pretend to be sick.

"The thing is, Coral . . . I'm not feeling very good." I fake-coughed.

"That's weird. You weren't coughing before," Coral said.

I shrugged my shoulders and fake-sniffled. I felt bad about lying to Coral, but I couldn't think of another way to quit working on the skit all afternoon.

"You don't sound too good, Dylan," said Coral. "Maybe we should just watch movies, or something. I could make you hot chocolate for your throat."

I nodded my head. At the moment, movies sounded better than mermaids.

9
EXPLORING OTHER SHORES

I was getting ready for camp on Monday morning when Coral called me on the computer.

"I have a bad cold," Coral said in a stuffy voice. Her body lurched toward her webcam as she let out a huge sneeze. I could almost feel the wet spray shooting out of my computer screen. Coral grabbed a tissue and honked her nose.

"How are *you* feeling, Dylan?" Coral said. "I must have caught it from you on Saturday."

I froze. I was supposed to be sick too. "Um . . . I feel better now." I faked a tiny cough. I felt too guilty to keep pretending. Especially when Coral was sick for real.

ART UNDER THE SEA!
SUMMER YOUTH ARTS CAMP

WORKSHOP SCHEDULE FOR
GROUP B: WEEK TWO

RECYCLED ART	DRAMA	WORKSHOP CHOICE	WORKSHOP CHOICE	ART SET-UP IN EXHIBIT HALL
BREAK	BREAK	BREAK	BREAK	BREAK
FILM	OCEAN MOVIES!	WORKSHOP CHOICE	PROP MAKING & PRACTICE	FINAL BACKSTAGE PREP
LUNCH	LUNCH	LUNCH	LUNCH	LUNCH
PROP MAKING & PRACTICE	PROP MAKING & PRACTICE	PROP MAKING & PRACTICE	DRESS REHEARSAL!	SHOWCASE!
GROUP GAMES	GROUP GAMES	GROUP GAMES	SWIMMING	FAREWELL PARTY

"My mom says I have a slight fever," Coral said. "I won't be at camp today."

"Oh. That's too bad," I said. It wouldn't be the same at camp without Coral. Who would I hang around with?

Coral explained some new ideas she had for our Mermaid Warrior Squad skit. "Oh! And I have the best idea about how the prop makers can create Mermaid Rock! You know that old office chair in the art studio, the one with the busted arm rest . . ." In her stuffy voice, Coral described a moveable Mermaid Rock on wheels. ". . . and you can get the prop makers started on it today!"

But I was only half-listening. It suddenly hit me — if Coral wasn't at camp, we couldn't work on the Mermaid Warrior Squad skit. And what if Coral was still sick tomorrow? We'd miss out on two whole days of practice. We'd have no choice but to forget about the whole thing! It's not like I wanted Coral to be sick or anything, but . . .

"Make sure you take your time getting better," I said.

"Thanks," said Coral. "See you tomorrow!"

She signed off with another big sneeze. It sounded almost as loud as her elephant seal roar.

After our morning workshops, we had time to work on our showcase projects. At first, I wasn't sure what to do without Coral. In the end, I decided to help make sea-themed props. But I didn't bother telling anyone to make Mermaid Rock. If Coral were away for a few days, there would be no skit anyway. Making Mermaid Rock would be a big waste of time.

Near the end of the day, Kelsey came up to me. "Hey, Dylan," she said. "Lynn volunteered to organize the backstage area. Would you like to join her?"

"Sure," I said right away. I guess Kelsey could tell I was bored working all by myself.

I walked with her to the theatre building. Then she showed me to one of the wings, where Lynn was sorting through some boxes. "Lynn, can you explain to Dylan what we're doing back here?" Kelsey asked. She told us she'd check in on us later to see how things were going.

"Hi, Dylan," said Lynn in her soft voice. She had a clipboard beside her and was wearing a wireless headset. She looked like a real theatre worker.

"Is that on?" I asked pointing to her head.

"Not right now. I'm just wearing it to get used to it for the show." She adjusted the black foam microphone in front of her mouth. "I'm helping Kelsey with the stage manager job. I'm going to make sure the actors get out on stage at the right time and have the right props."

"Cool," I said. It sounded like a neat job. Lynn would have the fun of being part of the show, but without standing on the stage where she might forget her lines or trip or make a mistake. If she did mess something up, the audience wouldn't know it was her fault. But I couldn't see Lynn messing up.

"We have four more boxes to go through," Lynn said. "Take these two and I'll take the others. I'm sorting everything. So far I have Wigs, Fish Puppets, Scenery, Boy Costumes, Girl Costumes . . ." Lynn pointed to neat piles beside the boxes as she read off the words on her list. "After that, we're going to help Kelsey figure out which skit they belong to and where to store them." Lynn had a big smile on her face, like organizing props was the best job in the world.

I knelt in front of my first box and opened it up to find the stuff we all had been making the week before. There were foam cylinders painted to look like broken pillars from an ancient underwater city. There was a cardboard treasure chest painted to look like old wood. It was bursting with what looked like heaps of shiny coins and colourful, glittering jewels. Of course, there were fish in different sizes, colours and materials — papier maché, cardboard and shiny cloth stuffed with soft cotton. The props made a thousand stories fire in my brain . . . *a city lost below the waves . . . a band of explorers discovering an enchanted underwater land . . .*

CRASH IS RUSHING INTO DANGER, JUST LIKE BEFORE.

I HAVE TO SAVE THE SEA . . . MY OWN WAY!

When I opened my second box, I gasped. I pulled out a perfect pirate captain hat made of rich black velvet. There was a long wispy white feather stuck in its side. It was beautiful, like something from a movie.

"Who made this?" I asked.

Lynn looked up. "A theatre group donated some costumes for the show. They did a pirate play last year."

I plopped the hat on my head to see what it felt like. The brim slipped down and covered my eyes. I put it aside and pulled a red velvet hat out of the box. The same thing happened when I put it on. I pushed up the brim and turned to Lynn. "I hope our actors have huge heads!"

Lynn pursed her lips. "They can stuff cloth in the hats if they're too big."

"Okay," I said taking off the red hat. "Good idea."

I watched Lynn as she bent over her clipboard and wrote, GET CLOTH TO STUFF HATS in big letters on her list. Lynn and Coral were very different from each other.

If Coral were working backstage, she wouldn't be making careful notes on a list. By now, she'd be dressed in a full pirate costume, twirling a sword in the air, and shouting in a pirate voice!

I turned back to the costume box. The deeper I dug, the more I was amazed. There were wide belts with big square buckles, and velvet vests with gold buttons. There were even black eye patches and shiny silver "hook" hands. I wondered what it would be like to go on stage dressed in something this nice. Would it make me less afraid of the audience?

One thing was for sure — it would beat wearing a shower curtain!

10
DRIFTING AWAY . . .

Coral was sick again on Tuesday. I missed her at camp, but I noticed I began to relax. There was no way we could do her Mermaid Warrior Squad skit now. We'd lost too much time. And it wouldn't be my fault at all! We could go back to working on our comic book in the morning and making props in the afternoon.

That afternoon, some of the campers started practising on the stage. I worked in the wing with Lynn again. We were going to arrange all the props in order for the show. We met with Kelsey to plan.

"Dylan and I saw a set of cubbies backstage,"

Lynn told Kelsey. "If it's okay, we could use them for storing the smaller props. We'll arrange them in the order of the skits. Left to right and top to bottom."

"That's a great idea, girls!" said Kelsey.

"I could clean up that corner over there," I said. "That's where we could keep the bigger things that won't fit in the cubby holes."

"You girls are so smart and organized," said Kelsey. She helped us push the cubby organizer nearer to the stage and suggested we label each cubby with the skit name. "There's a label maker in the other room — I'll get it for you." Lynn's eyes grew bright, like she'd just received a great birthday present.

I enjoyed cleaning up and organizing the offstage area. I carefully dusted out each of the cubbies. Then Lynn and I shared the label maker to mark every prop's storage place. After that, I found a broom and dustpan and swept the floor.

"Remember — more stuff will be coming in all week," Lynn said. "Let's be sure to leave room." She checked another item off on her list.

"Got it," I said. I felt good knowing we were helping the show run smoothly. Maybe I could work backstage full time, even when Coral did come back to camp. She and I could still hang out in the mornings.

"Is there a mirror back here?" A girl's voice blasted into our work area. It was Jade. She was dressed in a sparkly black top and a shiny silver skirt over dancer's tights. Sarina was right behind her in the same outfit.

"Why are you wearing that thing on your head," Jade said, eyeing Lynn's headset. "Are you in charge or something?"

"I'm Kelsey's assistant stage manager," said Lynn in her soft voice.

Jade didn't look impressed. "Well, do you know if there's a mirror back here?"

"Um . . . you're supposed to do your hair and makeup in the dressing room," Lynn replied.

Jade crossed her arms. "Well, the dressing room is locked. Right, Sarina?"

Sarina nodded. But I saw that she was embarrassed by Jade's rudeness.

"Today's not the dress rehearsal," said Lynn. "So you don't need to be all dressed up and in makeup today." I looked closer. Sure enough, both Jade and Sarina were wearing sparkly eyeshadow and dark eyeliner.

Jade threw her hands in the air. Then she turned her head and looked at me. She raised one eyebrow. "Are you the cleaning lady?"

A lump rose in my throat. I felt my palms grow sweaty on the broom handle. Just looking at Jade reminded me of the mean things she'd said about my hair that first day.

So I shocked myself when words tumbled from my mouth. "I saw a mirror," I heard myself say. "It's over there by the other shelves."

"Where?" Jade demanded.

I shuffled over to the spot. The mirror wasn't easy to get to. There was a stack of things piled high in front of it.

"That's a dumb place for it," said Jade. "We'll have to move it."

"We have to ask Kelsey before we move things like that around," Lynn said. "Not

everything back here is for our show."

I saw Jade narrow her eyes and glare at Lynn.

"Don't worry, Jade. You look great," said Sarina. "Same as in the bathroom two minutes ago."

"But I could *barely* see the mirror in there. The lights were too dim." Jade fluffed up her perfect ponytail. "Think how packed the dressing room will be on the day of the show, Sarina. It's going to be a *disaster*!"

"I think you both look really nice," I said. My heart started to beat faster. My nerves were wiggling.

"Thanks," said Sarina.

Jade sent another poison glance at Lynn who had gone back to work on the cubbies. Then she turned to me. "Are you just the backstage sweeper?"

I shook my head. "No," I said. "I'm helping to get this wing organized for the show."

"Are you going to be back here for all the rehearsals and the actual show?"

"I don't know," I said. Well, I didn't.

Jade's face suddenly relaxed. The poison look left her eyes. "You could help us. I know *she* won't," she lowered her voice and nodded toward Lynn. "Maybe you could take down this mirror and stash it somewhere? Then we could ask you for it when we needed it."

Part of me wanted to walk away from Jade. But the other part wanted to do something for her.

"You said you're organizing things, right?" said Jade. "The dressing room is going to get really busy for the show. It would make sense to have more room for getting ready."

I thought about it. If I organized things just right by the mirror, it might help everyone get ready on time. "I could clean this stuff up. I don't think Kelsey would mind that," I said. "I think I saw a tall stool somewhere in the back. I could set it up in front of the mirror for people to sit on." I pictured the new area in my head. I could turn it into a cute, mini dressing room.

"Could you find a little table too? Maybe something that has a drawer for our makeup tools?" Jade asked. "That way we don't have to carry them around all the time."

"I have some ideas. I'll talk to Lynn about it," I said.

"Or . . . what about just doing it yourself, Dylan," said Jade. "I don't think *she'd* get it. Also," she lowered her voice to a whisper, "once you set it all up, could you make sure to save it for us?"

"How?" I heard myself whisper back, like we were planning a secret mission.

"Oh, I don't know. Maybe you could guard it or something. Just until our dance number starts."

"You're on video!" Ben's voice burst into the room.

It was silly, but I felt my heart thump, like I'd been caught stealing something.

"Turn it off," giggled Jade. "We're not ready!" But she gave Ben a huge grin.

I watched as Ben kept filming. Jade and Sarina struck poses and gave the camera their most glamorous model smiles.

11
OCEANS APART

The next morning, my stomach did a flip-flop when Coral stepped out of her mom's car. She was wearing her shower curtain fishtail over her shorts.

"Hey there, Driftwood!" Coral shouted. "Ready for Mermaid Warriors to go live?"

I was about to respond when Coral said, "Hey, where's your MWS bracelet?" She pointed at my bare wrist.

"I couldn't find it this morning," I said. It wasn't on my bookshelf where I thought I'd left it the night before. I didn't say that I didn't look very hard for it after that.

"All right. We can make you another one later," Coral said. "Anyway, did you tell the prop makers our ideas for making Mermaid Rock? I can't wait to see it!"

"Uh . . . no," I said. "I didn't tell them."

"Oh, okay. We can tell them together. Also, I wrote a script for a voice-over. I thought we could ask Morgan to record it in his deep actor voice . . ." Coral stopped talking. She must have noticed the funny look I felt forming on my face.

"Oh, no — you're not sick again, are you, Dylan?" Coral asked.

"No," I said, my voice barely a whisper.

"PHEW!" Coral boomed. "I thought for a minute that you might not be able to do our skit!"

I took a deep breath, then quickly said. "We're not doing the skit."

"What do you mean?"

"I mean *we're not doing the skit*. How can we? There's hardly any time left to practise. We don't even have our props."

"There's *really* lots of time!" Coral said.

"I bet we can finish our props today. All we really need is Mermaid Rock, anyway. Then we just have to learn two or three lines each and practise our warrior moves. It's easy!"

I stared at Coral. How did I ever believe that we shared a brain?

"Everyone else has been practising all week," I tried to explain. "And their props look amazing. And . . ." I took another breath, "I promised Kelsey that I would help work backstage."

Coral shook her head. "But she can just find someone else, right?"

"I don't want them to find someone else. I *like* working backstage."

"But, Dylan — you're Driftwood!" Coral laughed. "You *have* to do the skit!"

She bumped her shoulder into mine. I wobbled sideways and almost fell over. As I looked around to see if anyone was watching, I felt a wave of anger ripple through me.

"No, I don't *have* to, Coral," I said. "And I didn't ask to do the dorky skit in the first place!"

Her smile vanished. "I can't believe you just

called our Mermaid Warriors *dorky*."

I squirmed. "I mean, I like our comic book. But the skit was all your idea — you didn't even ask me."

"But . . . we'd have so much fun," Coral said.

"Maybe you would, but not me."

"I don't get it, Dylan! You come up with all these great ideas, but you never want to share them. Isn't that why we made up Crash and Driftwood, to have fun sharing them?"

"Why can't we just share our comic book pages?" I asked. "Why isn't that enough? I don't like being laughed at!" My voice was rising. "I don't want people pointing at our dumb moves and our junky costumes and laughing their heads off . . ."

"Fine!" Coral said. "I'm going to do our skit. I don't know about you, but I *really* believe in Mermaid Warrior Squad."

Coral turned and walked away.

"'Predator Vs. Prey' is next," said Lynn, listening to Kelsey through her headset. It was the dress rehearsal, so there were people in the audience — other kids and instructors from camp.

My job was to locate Bob. I handed the shark to Lamar as he got to the entrance of the stage. Ryan rolled out their mini puppet theatre.

I noticed that Lamar's hands were shaking.

"Are you nervous?" I whispered.

"A bit," he said. "More excited than nervous."

"Break a leg," I said. Morgan had taught us that actors say that instead of "good luck."

Lamar grinned, then stepped on stage. He swooshed Bob through the air to the rhythm of the low, rumbling music.

I could see a bit of the stage from where I stood. I could hear the audience hoot and laugh as Lamar and Ryan practised their show. "Hey, Dylan, we used the mirror," said Jade. She and Sarina walked up to me, ready to rehearse their dance.

"We covered it up again with that sheet," said Sarina.

"Hiding it like that was a good idea," said Jade, giving me a wink. "You'll do that for the show too — right?"

I nodded. I hadn't planned to cover the little makeup area just for Jade and Sarina. But I couldn't spend all my time guarding it with everything else I was doing. And Lynn didn't know about the mini dressing room. I'd put it together when she was busy and I wasn't sure she'd like it.

Ben sidled up to us. "You've got to watch this," I heard him whisper to Jade. He pointed his camera at the puppet show. Suddenly, there was a clunk that didn't sound quite right, then another, then another. I looked out and saw Ryan holding his school of fish puppets. Their heads had all popped off and landed on the stage!

"Good prank!" Jade whispered to Ben. I felt really bad for Ryan and Lamar. I wondered if they'd stop the show and walk off stage.

But instead of being embarrassed, they kept going. Lamar made Bob gulp up the headless fish. "Fish heads give me gas, anyway!" said Lamar in Bob's rumbly voice. The audience laughed even harder and the puppet show went on. Ben looked disappointed as he shut off his camera.

"'Tidal Wave Crush' — you're up!" said Lynn pointing to Jade and Sarina.

"Thanks, Ms. Headset," I heard Jade murmur to Ben.

The two dancing divas went out on stage. Their music started to play. Jade and Sarina twisted, turned and jumped in perfect sync, like they'd practised a million times. They probably had. When they finished every amazing move, the crowd went crazy with cheers, and it wasn't even the real show!

"'Mermaid Warrior Squad' is next," I heard Lynn say when the dance was over. That was my cue.

I walked over to where the Mermaid Rock prop was stashed. It really did look like an underwater rock. I'd seen Coral working on it with the instructor. It was an old rolling chair covered with a grey sheet. Underneath the sheet were cushions arranged to give the rock lumps and bumps. The instructor had added green seaweed, and spray-painted shadows to make it look real.

"Now, Dylan!" Lynn said in a loud whisper. I rolled Mermaid Rock onto the stage. I felt the heat of the spotlight. The floor felt slick beneath my feet and I worried I'd slip. What if Ben was filming? Then I glanced out into the theatre and sucked in my breath. The audience was all watching *me*! My heart started thudding in my chest like a drum. I set up Mermaid Rock as quickly as I could, then rushed back to the wing with my head ducked low.

I was in the wing taking deep breaths when Morgan's voice began to play over the speakers: "In the depths of the ocean, two Mermaid Warriors defend the sea. They fight the polluting ways of Captain Fishhead and his evil minions, the Seaweed Sisters . . ."

Coral stomped onto the stage in her homemade Crash costume. I guess she had time to get Mermaid Rock or a new costume made, not both. The underwater video with the boat began to play. Coral kicked, punched and battled like a Mermaid Warrior!

"Why aren't you out there with her?" asked Lamar, coming up beside me. "It doesn't make any sense when she's by herself." Jade, Sarina and Ben were huddled together laughing quietly, while Ben filmed Coral.

With only one actor, the skit was short, even though Coral paused where Driftwood's lines were supposed to be. Soon Coral said Crash's final line. "WE DID IT!" she boomed. Then she hopped back to sit on Mermaid Rock.

Swoosh!

Mermaid Rock shot out from under her and went skidding across the stage.

Thud!

Coral tumbled toward the stage and landed hard on her rear. People in the audience gasped. Then Kelsey ran out onto the stage to see if Coral was okay.

I looked at Ben. But he was shaking his head.

BUT IT'S THE EVIL SEAWEED SISTERS IN DISGUISE ... WHAT ARE THEY UP TO?

HEY! WANT TO COME TO A BEACH PARTY?

IT'S GOING TO BE SO MUCH FUN!

SWIPE

EVERYONE WILL BE THERE ...

SZZZT

YOU SHOULD REALLY COME ALONG!

SZZZT

"Who thought of that one? That was *awesome*!" He looked surprised at what had just happened.

"Now we know why she calls herself Crash," Jade laughed.

Lynn dashed over to me. "Did you lock the wheels?" she asked.

"I . . . think so," I said. But my nerves were wiggling. I'd locked some of them for sure — but I'd also been in a rush to get off the stage.

What if Coral was hurt and it was my fault?

12
SINK OR SWIM?

After the dress rehearsal, I did my best to keep avoiding Coral. Besides our fight about the skit, I had another reason to stay out of her way. What if she blamed me for the accident on stage?

I knew Coral was fine because right after her fall she had leaped to her feet and shouted, "CRASH IS OKAY, FOLKS!" She had done a funny little tap dance to show that nothing was sprained or sore. Then she had bowed and walked off the stage. But how could she not be upset with me now?

It was harder than I thought it would be to avoid Coral. When our group went to the pool for one last swim, I was by myself. And everywhere I looked, there was Coral — doing handstands in the shallow end, swimming laps in the middle pool. When I walked toward the diving boards, I spotted Coral already heading there with Lamar and Ryan. They were shouting dares at each other to do twists and backward jumps. I hung back and stood by the edge of the water. I felt my damp skin break out in goosebumps.

"Hey, Dylan, want to hang out with us?" said a voice from below. I looked at Jade and Sarina in the pool. They were hanging over the edge of a floating raft.

I looked around to make sure Ben wasn't filming. Maybe someone was planning to push me in as a joke.

"Okay," I finally said. I lowered myself into the water. It was better than shivering by the side of the pool. There was no more room on their raft, so I treaded water beside them.

"We have to stay on the raft to keep our hair dry," Jade explained. She and Sarina were still wearing their hair like they did at the dress rehearsal, in high, bouncy ponytails. I could even see traces of silver glitter in Jade's curls.

"I don't mind swimming," I said.

I felt Jade eyeing my hair. "Have you ever tried some colour?" Jade asked. "Maybe purple bangs."

I felt funny as Jade stared at my head. Was she still making fun of my hair? Was she laughing inside and trying to tell me how to be more girly? Or could it be that she was really starting to like me? "Maybe," was all I said.

Jade leaned one arm on the raft and turned to Sarina. She started talking about their dance number. Jade gave Sarina lots of advice on how to do better turns and jumps for the dance.

"And remember — *wait* one beat before our first step," Jade lectured. "Or you'll throw the whole dance off, like you did last time."

I saw Sarina bite her lower lip. But she didn't say anything back to Jade.

Just then, I felt a current swish past me and a big spray of water hit me right in the face!

"Gotcha!"

I squeezed my eyes shut and coughed. I opened my eyes to see Ben, of course. He grinned, then turned to splash Jade and Sarina. They giggled and splashed him back with weak, flirty splashes. Then Ben grabbed Jade by the arm and pulled her off the raft. Jade fake-screamed, but you could tell she was having a blast. It looked like she'd forgotten all about protecting her hair too.

Sarina invited me to join her on the raft. I swam over and hoisted myself up. We watched as Ben and Jade pushed and chased each other. Sarina looked just as bored as I felt.

"So are you and Coral enemies now?" Sarina asked.

"No," I said. I hoped Coral didn't think I was her enemy.

"I didn't think so. That's what I told Jade," said Sarina quietly. I wondered why she and Jade were talking about Coral and me.

"But you're not in her skit," Sarina continued. "Why not?"

I was surprised. Wasn't it obvious? Hadn't Sarina laughed with Jade and Ben whenever Coral became Crash?

"I don't know," I said. "It's embarrassing in spots. I don't like getting laughed at."

Sarina shrugged. "Coral doesn't mind when people laugh. She's always doing crazy things at school."

No kidding! I thought.

"Sometimes she's weird. But I think she's pretty funny," Sarina added. Maybe Coral was right. Maybe Sarina only acted like a Jade in front of people like Jade.

"I really like your comic book, by the way. It's creative," said Sarina. Her voice sounded almost shy. "It's not the usual mermaid stuff."

"Well, I think your dance is amazing." My voice was shy too. "I know Jade says it needs more practice, but . . ."

Sarina shrugged. "It's the same dance we did for our dance academy recital. We won a trophy for it, so we've already done it a million times. But Jade *always* thinks we need more practice." I thought it was funny that Sarina and I had the opposite problem with our friends. Coral never practised, and Jade never stopped!

Jade and Ben swam up to us, out of breath. They seemed to have finished their flirty game.

"Hey, Sarina. I was telling Ben about our *plan*." Jade sent Sarina a winking look. "Don't you think it's time to ask her?" She jutted her chin toward me.

"Ask me what?" I said. I didn't like the weird smile forming on Jade's lips, or the glint in Ben's eyes.

"I don't think we should," said Sarina. I felt her squirm on the raft. "They're really not enemies, you know."

"Whatever!" Jade laughed and looked at me. "Hey, Dylan — want to help us do another prank on Coral at the showcase?"

Another prank?

"Do you mean when she fell?" I asked. "That was an accident."

"Yeah, right," said Ben. "Aren't you the one who pushed that Mermaid Rock thing on stage?"

I felt a surge of panic. Did everyone think I'd played a trick on Coral? All this time I was scared Coral would blame me for messing up by accident. But what if she believed I'd done it on purpose? It was worse than I thought!

"Even if it was an accident, it was hilarious," said Jade. "And we thought of something better." Her sideways grin at Ben gave me a fresh set of goosebumps. "You're the perfect one to booby trap that Mermaid Rock prop."

I shook my head. "No way. Coral could get hurt." I thought of the loud thud as Coral crashed down onto the stage.

"We're not going to mess with the wheels this time," Jade explained.

"It would be better if the chair stood still," said Ben.

"What are you guys planning?" I was worried about what Coral must think of me, but I knew I had to pay attention. Maybe I could warn her!

"We're going to make a bunch of water balloons," Jade explained. "And *you* can stick them under the grey blanket right before you wheel Mermaid Rock on stage."

I could see it now. Coral hopping back onto the seat and — *SPLOOSH!* — she'd be soaked. She'd look like she'd wet her pants — in front of everyone! If that happened to me, I just know I would *die*. Not only that . . .

"But . . . what if the floor gets wet?" I asked. "What if Coral slips and hurts herself? What about the rest of the people on stage?" The smooth stage floor was slick even when it was perfectly dry. I thought of how easily Mermaid Rock shot across the stage when Coral tried to sit on it. Add a puddle of water and it might be as slippery as ice!

"Dylan's right," said Sarina. "If anyone got hurt, we'd all be in big trouble."

"Coral's *not* going to slip. She's just going to get a soaking," said Jade rolling her eyes. "And who's going to say it was us, anyway?"

"But . . . everyone will make fun." In my mind I could see Coral leaving the stage with a sopping wet backside as everyone hooted and laughed.

"That's the point of a prank," said Ben. "Come on — it will be awesome!"

Jade glared at me. "So, you're *not* going to help us?"

No way! I thought. But all I did was shrug.

"Well, don't even think of telling her," said Ben. "Or we'll plan something worse."

13
DANGER AT HIGH TIDE!

"I'm going to organize the big props for the pirate skit," Lynn told me. She glanced at her clipboard. "Can you check the cubbies to make sure all the pirate belts are there?"

"Just a second," I said. I was near Mermaid Rock. Ben and Jade weren't around, so I could make sure it wasn't booby-trapped. *So far so good — no water balloons!*

All the sneaking around while trying to do my job for the showcase was stressful! But in the end, I decided it was better than telling Coral. I could picture her flying into a rage, chasing down Ben and Jade, and screaming for justice! And then . . . who knows what kind of scheme Ben and Jade would cook up! They didn't even care if the tricks they pulled hurt someone.

No, I had to do this my own way. If I found water balloons, I'd hide them before wheeling Mermaid Rock on stage. Maybe I could even sneak the balloons back after the skit . . . let Ben and Jade think their water balloons hadn't worked when Coral sat down. At least no one would make a big scene, and no one would get embarrassed or hurt.

After checking on the pirate belts, I made my way back to my spot at the entrance to the stage. "Did you hear the crowd?" Lamar whispered to me as he and Ryan came off the stage. Lamar was holding Bob, and Ryan was pushing the puppet theatre. This time, all the puppet heads were firmly connected.

"'Predator vs. Prey' was a hit!" said Ryan. I could hear the audience still cheering for their puppet show. I peeked out into the crowd. The plush chairs were packed with other campers and families. I even recognized Coral's mom in the front row.

As I scanned the crowd to find my dad, a sharp voice behind me made me jump. "Dylan!" I turned around to face Jade. My stomach lurched like I was on a rollercoaster. Had she seen me peeking at Mermaid Rock?

"Where's our makeup spot?" she demanded.

That was what she wanted — of course! The only thing on her mind was getting perfect for the dance number. Maybe she was so focused on that, she'd forgotten about soaking Coral.

"Same place as always," I mumbled. With everything else going on, I forgot to cover it with the sheet. But I didn't mention that.

"It's not there," Jade complained. "Someone moved the stool and the table. I put my brushes and my fancy glitter lipstick in the drawer. And now it's all *gone!*"

"It's okay, Jade," said Sarina. "No one's going to notice our lipstick. Let's just do our dance."

"Well make sure you don't mess *that* up too!" Jade snapped meanly. I saw Sarina wince.

Lynn came toward us, "'Tidal Wave Crush' dancers — you're on in thirty seconds!"

"We *know*!" Jade said. "But I can't find my glitter lipstick. I left it in the little table!"

Lynn shook her head. "That table by the mirror? I moved it back into the dressing room."

"Why did you do that? I don't have time to go back there!" Jade cried.

"It's my job to put everything back in its proper place," Lynn said. "Or there could be chaos."

"UGH! You're such a dork, Ms. Headset!" Jade looked ready to burst. But then we heard the first few notes of "Tidal Wave Crush." Jade and Sarina had to get out on stage — *fast*.

"So, Dylan. What's the best part of working backstage?" Ryan asked, pointing his camera at me. He spoke in a very soft voice as he recorded video for the camp documentary. I agreed to do the interview, as long as it was short. I shoved my hands in my hoodie pockets. (I saw a video of myself once where I kept clenching and unclenching my fingers because I was nervous. It made me look weird.)

"Um . . . the best part is helping out, I guess," I replied in a voice just above a whisper. On stage, Jade and Sarina's dance music was so loud, there's no way anyone in the audience could hear us. But we were being quiet, just in case.

"What sort of things do you help out with?"

I told Ryan about organizing the props and handing the right things to the performers. As I talked, the fingers on my right hand bumped into something in my pocket. I felt the rubbery loops and the round metal disk. It was my MWS bracelet, the one I thought I'd lost!

"But there's one thing I don't understand," Ryan went on. "It's so fun being on stage. Don't you ever feel you're missing out?"

Before I could answer, Kelsey appeared with a serious look on her face.

"Dylan — I need your help," she said. *"Walrus prop malfunction!"*

I looked over at Lynn. She whispered, "Go with Kelsey — I'll take over for you."

"And I'll film you," said Ryan to me, his video rolling. "*Backstage work in action!*"

We followed Kelsey to the large stuffed walrus prop for the Arctic Sea dance number. One of its tusks had fallen off and was lying beside it on the floor. I wondered if this was another one of Ben's pranks. If it was, it had gone off early!

"Can you hold Wally steady, Dylan? I'll try to put him back together." Kelsey dropped to her knees while I cradled the walrus's squishy foam head in my arms.

Ryan filmed while Kelsey poked and twisted the tusk into place. As I stood there, I saw something shiny out of the corner of my eye. I looked in the direction of the sparkles. . . Oh, no. I didn't hear music anymore, so Jade and Sarina's dance must have ended. Sure enough, there was Jade in her glittery costume standing right near Mermaid Rock.

"You have to stand still, Dylan," Kelsey said.

My heart began to pound. It was hard to

tell, but was Jade reaching into her bulging backpack?

I squinted my eyes for a better look. It looked like Jade was taking something from her backpack and stuffing it under the grey blanket! And Ben was standing beside her with his camera recording.

"Um . . . Kelsey . . ." I started. But a group of Arctic Sea dancers suddenly crowded around us. They chattered at us, checking to see if the walrus surgery would be finished in time for their dance. Kelsey told everyone to be quiet and patient as she reattached the tusk.

"There!" Kelsey finally said. As soon as she was done, she left to help one of the Arctic dancers with his costume. I'd have to deal with Mermaid Rock myself.

I pushed past the crowd of dancers and dashed toward Mermaid Rock. But it wasn't there! Lynn had already wheeled it on stage.

Coral's skit was moments away.

14
TAKING THE PLUNGE!

I raced to the edge of the stage. I watched Coral, dressed as Crash, "swim" onto the stage from the other side. I heard someone in the audience hoot and clap as Coral made her appearance. It was Coral's mom in the front row! My stomach flip-flopped. She was going to see Coral get pranked too.

I tried sending thoughts in Coral's direction: *Watch out for Mermaid Rock! Booby trap! BOOBY TRAP!* I wished Coral and I shared a brain for real.

As I stood there, I felt someone crash into me. I was nearly knocked down. It was a smallish person dressed a bit like a ninja on top . . . *with a shower curtain mermaid tail!*

"Sorry," he mumbled.

He?

"Lamar?" I said. I squinted at the brown eyes peeking out from the gap in his ninja headgear. "Is that you?"

"Ah, nuts," Lamar mumbled from behind the scarf covering his mouth. "I didn't think anyone could tell."

"Why are you . . . how did you . . . ?" I began. I was interrupted by Coral shouting, "Watch out for the mighty Crash!"

And suddenly — just like that — I knew how to save Coral! But I needed Lamar to go along. My heart thundered in my chest. I had about ten seconds to pull it off.

Now or never!

"Give me your costume," I demanded.

"Now?"

"NOW!" I said.

I didn't have time to explain — but I didn't need to. Lamar had already whipped off the

scarf and tail and shoved them in my hands.

"Be my guest," he said. He seemed fine with my going on stage instead of him.

As fast as I could, I tied the tail around my waist. Lucky thing I was wearing my black hoodie, so I arranged the scarf as ninja-like as possible on top of it. "Where is my Mermaid Warrior ally, Driftwood?" Coral's voice boomed.

That was my cue.

But a fresh wave of nerves wiggled through me. What was going to happen out there? Would I just make things worse? Would everyone point and laugh?

"So, are you going to go out there, or what?" Lamar asked.

I didn't answer. Instead, I shoved my hand in my pocket, grabbed my MWS bracelet, and pulled it onto my wrist. Then I stepped onto the stage and into the spotlight.

"I'm with you, Crash!" I shouted. "FOREVER SWIM!"

I dipped my arms into the air in front of me like Coral had done, to make it look like swimming. My legs were wobbly, but I forced them to take big strides as my tail swooshed. I joined Coral in the middle of the stage.

Coral froze when she saw it was me. We stood there doing nothing for a few seconds, but it felt like minutes . . . *hours* . . .

This was exactly what I was afraid of! I'd surprised Coral . . . and instead of saving her, I was going to make her flub the whole skit! I gulped as I felt hundreds of eyes on me.

Suddenly, Coral came to life. She boomed Crash's next line, "LET'S DO THIS THING!" Her body unfroze and flowed into a warrior pose.

Right on cue, the music grew louder. It was time for the epic finale!

Coral, as mighty Crash, mimed her warrior moves. I copied, trying my best to become Driftwood. Under the bright spotlights and with the music going, it was almost . . . fun.

I heard the audience laughing. But I could feel that it was a *good* kind of laugh. Like they were having fun too. Then the action music

stopped and the battle scene ended. Morgan's narrator voice thundered over the speakers: "It was an amazing victory for the brave Mermaid Warriors!"

That meant that it was time for Coral's last line. I had to act fast to put the most important part of my plan into action.

"WE DID IT!" Coral shouted, throwing her arms out to her sides.

She hopped backward onto Mermaid Rock, and I shot forward. I grabbed Coral's hands . . . I had to hold on and stop her from sitting down . . . when suddenly . . .

Slam!

Coral's backside plopped firmly onto Mermaid Rock . . .

. . . and nothing happened.

She was completely dry!

I felt a huge smile spread across my face.

I noticed that Coral's smile changed to a stare. She looked at me and coughed.

Then she coughed again, and nodded her chin toward her hands. I realized I was still squeezing them in mine. It wasn't part of the skit. The audience was staring at us, and no one was clapping. They were expecting something more.

When Coral coughed again, I realized what she was waiting for. Driftwood had the last line of the skit! What was it? I couldn't remember. And I had to say something to explain why I was holding Crash's hands.

Suddenly, as Driftwood, I shouted: "Yes, we did it, Crash! And now . . . DANCE PARTY TIME!"

I yanked Coral toward me, whipping her off of Mermaid Rock. A big laugh bubbled up from the audience.

"*What are you . . . ?*" Coral whispered.

I whispered back in Coral's ear, "*Go with the flow!*"

I spun us around and moved us across the stage. I tried to make it look like a victory dance was part of our skit.

The more everyone laughed, the more loose and comfortable Coral became. She even spun *me* around, then pressed her cheek against mine, like we were doing a tango. It was like energy flowed toward her from the audience and made her braver. I felt the audience energy too.

We were hand in hand, our arms stretched out in front of us, and our faces close together. And that's how we strutted right off the stage!

The audience applauded so loud, it sounded like thunder.

15
THE END OF THE
(FISH) TAIL

Backstage, I leaned against the wall. I was trying to catch my breath. I felt like I had just finished running the hundred-metre sprint. I wanted to laugh and cry and take a nap — all at the same time.

"I can't believe we actually did a tango!" Coral roared, then clapped her hand over her mouth. Another skit had started on stage.

"I'm . . . sorry . . . about the dance," I said in a soft voice between gulps of air. "I didn't know what else to do."

"Sorry?" Coral whispered back. "Why? That was *really* awesome. The audience cracked up!"

We both covered our mouths and laughed. We crept away from the stage so we could talk in normal voices. Lamar and Ryan shimmied up to us, doing their own tango — holding Bob in between them.

"We saw your sweet moves," said Lamar.

"Super funny!" added Ryan.

Coral grabbed my hands and we tangoed beside the boys.

I think I finally understood what I'd been seeing all through the showcase. Almost everyone seemed nervous before they went out on stage, then a bit kooky and giggly when they came off. Now I knew that going out there was like swimming into fear, but flowing right into fun.

"What happened, anyway?" Coral said when we finished dancing. "I thought Lamar was going to be Driftwood."

"Shh!" Lamar whispered, looking around. "Dylan can tell you — I was all dressed up and everything. She's the one who *made* me give her the costume. So you still have to give us the stuff."

"Of course! I'm not mad," said Coral. "I *really* did make like a dozen extra Shark Dude badges for your piñat —"

"SHHHHH!"

"I mean, for . . . *Bob*," Coral matched Lamar's whisper.

So Lamar had agreed to be a mermaid as a trade for Coral's homemade piñata prizes!

"But what about you, Dylan? When did you stop being afraid of the stage?" Coral asked.

"I didn't," I said.

"Then . . . what made you decide to be Driftwood again?"

I told Coral about Jade and Ben and the water balloon prank. After all, they couldn't do anything now.

"So, what you're saying is . . . *you came out there to save me!*" Coral boomed. Then she crushed me in a huge hug. "My *hero!*" she said in a loud, cartoonish voice. My cheeks felt warm, but I didn't really care. It was good to be friends with Coral again.

"Jade and Ben were going to soak you — in

front of everyone?" asked Ryan.

"Nasty!" added Lamar.

Coral scrunched her eyebrows. "But . . . there weren't any balloons. I landed right on the chair. I didn't feel anything."

"I know. I can't explain," I said. "I saw Jade do it. I even saw Ben filming the whole thing! Wanna check it?"

"Of course!"

We all headed to the corner where Lynn had stashed Mermaid Rock. Ryan flicked on the camera dangling from his wrist. I picked up the bottom edge of the grey blanket and yanked it off the chair. In front of us was just the regular old office chair with lumpy cushions and duct tape.

"Guess she didn't go through with it," I said. I bit my lip. It was a mystery.

Nearby, we heard angry words between a boy and a girl. Curious, we all headed in that direction. Jade and Ben were arguing, pointing fingers at each other, when . . .

. . . *SPLOOSH!*

A burst of water sloshed onto the floor.

THE END OF THE (FISH) TAIL

Jade shrieked and held her "SASSY" backpack away from her body, like it was contaminated. She was up on the tiptoes of her glittery dance shoes, like a car had zoomed past and splashed her. It kind of looked like one had — her feet were drenched! Busted water balloons lay in a puddle on the ground.

"What just . . ." Coral began, when — *SPLOOSH!* — another water balloon slid from the open flap of Jade's backpack and hit the floor. It broke at Ben's feet. He jumped back and threw himself off balance, dropping his camera right into the puddle!

Ben's face went from surprised to embarrassed as everyone turned to look. And his cheeks burned red when he spotted Ryan with his camera rolling, capturing the public soaking on video.

"You'd better delete that!" Ben said to Ryan. Then he turned to Jade. "Thanks a lot!" he growled.

"Why were these in here?" asked Jade. She looked at Sarina. "You put them back in my bag, didn't you?"

"I didn't touch them, Jade," said Sarina.

"Wait — did you say '*put them back*'?" Ryan asked, still filming. "So Jade, you admit it — *on camera* — you brought those balloons and put them somewhere."

Jade glared at Ryan. But, without meaning to, she had confessed her crime in front of everyone. Why bring a bag full of water balloons backstage except for a prank? She pointed at Ben. "It was his idea."

Ben gave her a nasty scowl.

"What happened here? It's all wet!" It was Kelsey. She looked at Jade and Ben. Anyone could see that they looked guilty. "Is that one of the camp's cameras on the floor?" Kelsey bent down to pick up Ben's camera. "I'll have to give it a good check to make sure it's not broken."

Ben's eyes went wide. "Are you going to look at what's on it?" he asked.

"Of course," said Kelsey. "That's how I'll know if it's still working."

Ben looked more scared than embarrassed now. If the camera was broken, he'd be in trouble. And even if it wasn't, Kelsey would see that Ben had been using the camera to film his dumb pranks and jokes all week.

Meanwhile, Lynn showed up with a bucket and a stack of dry cloths.

"I'll clean up," she said.

"Thanks, Lynn," Kelsey said. She looked at the wet camera in her hand, then said to Jade and Ben, "I think you two should come with me." As the three of them walked away, Lynn knelt near the wet spot on the floor. She started to sop up the water with a cloth.

"We'll help you," I said.

"Thanks," Lynn said. She handed a cloth each to Coral and me. We knelt down beside her. As we all picked up stray broken balloon bits and mopped up the puddle, Coral turned to me. "I still don't get how the water balloons ended up in Jade's bag if you saw her put them in Mermaid Rock."

I was about to agree when I saw a tiny smile form on Lynn's usually serious face. Suddenly, the pieces of the prank puzzle fit together.

"Hmm," I said. "I wonder, Coral. It's such a strange mystery. Do *you* know anything about it, Lynn?"

Lynn shrugged. She gathered the wet cloths into the bucket and stood up.

"It's my job to put everything back in its proper place," Lynn said.

I knew it!

"Or there might be chaos, right?" I said with a grin.

Lynn smiled and nodded as she walked away.

Coral asked, "What was that *really* supposed to mean?"

"I'll tell you all about it," I said.

ACKNOWLEDGEMENTS

Like Dylan, I also dreamed of one day becoming either an author or a marine biologist (specializing in sharks, of course). I'm busy working on the first dream, and am grateful to my family, friends and readers for their enthusiastic support. I'd like to offer a huge thank you to all the talented people who made this super-cool, hybrid novel/comic book possible, especially to my fellow 'creative squad members' Kat Mototsune and Janine Carrington. (As for that second dream of mine, I'm still gathering the courage to hop into a shark cage!)

— Karin

I'd like to thank my beautiful, spunky, amazing son Luis-Mario for being so patient, eager to please, and fun. Thank you to my mom, Kat and Karin for being such enthusiastic and supportive co-creatives, my friend Sophia Roach for introducing me to Kat and Karin, and God — all of whom are responsible for giving me the opportunity to help bring such a cool story to life.

— Janine